SPLASH IT UP!

★ ☆

AUDITIONS TODAY

A MERMAID COMES TO
NEW YORK AND TAKES
THE BUSINESS WORLD
BY STORM!

To Gillian Sore and Clare Whitston
(The Queens of Storyland), Alex McNabb and Iain Martin
(Chief Glitterers), Tracy Donnelly, Annabel Kantaria,
Lucy Strange and Charlotte Butterfield
(Cupcake Decorators), Wayne Jordan and Jack Cheshire
(Rainbow Polishers) and Abbie, Darius, Emily and
Kelsey (Unicorn Racing Enthusiasts)

OXFORD
UNIVERSITY PRESS

Great Clarendon Street, Oxford OX2 6DP
Oxford University Press is a department of the University of Oxford.
It furthers the University's objective of excellence in research, scholarship,
and education by publishing worldwide. Oxford is a registered trade mark of
Oxford University Press in the UK and in certain other countries

First published 2017

British Library Cataloguing in Publication Data
Data available

ISBN: 978-0-19-274714-3

1 3 5 7 9 10 8 6 4 2

Printed in Great Britain
Paper used in the production of this book is a natural,
recyclable product made from wood grown in sustainable forests.
The manufacturing process conforms to the environmental
regulations of the country of origin.

All other photographs copyright © Shutterstock

UNICORN IN NEW YORK

LOUIE
MAKES
A
SPLASH!

RACHEL HAMILTON

Illustrated by Oscar Armelles

OXFORD
UNIVERSITY PRESS

Chapter One

Greetings

Greetings, humans. It's me, Louie the Unicorn, and I'm back once again to say, 'LOVE ME!'

Oops. Sorry. Bit overexcited. What I *meant* to say was . . . Greetings, humans. It's me, Louie the Unicorn, and I'm back once again to say, 'LISTEN TO ME!' Because I'm here to share another thrilling tale of drama, destiny, and DIVAS (that would be you, Miranda the Mermaid) from the New York School of Performing Arts.

This time, our adventure began outside the John Feelgood Theatre, queuing to audition for *Splash it Up!*—the hottest new show in town from the world-famous musical theatre producers, Andrew Velvet-Curtains and Tim Dry-Ice.

Splash it Up! was creating a huge buzz in the entertainment world and an even bigger buzz in Miranda the Mermaid's tank as we read the audition poster aloud for the thousandth time:

Splash it up!

A mermaid comes to New York and takes the business world by storm.

'It's perfect!' Frank the Troll burped with delight and pirouetted on the spot. 'This part could have been written for you, Miranda.'

I clapped my hooves in agreement. 'There is only one superstar, super-singing mermaid in this city. You were born to make a "splash", Miranda.'

'♫Oooh♫,' Miranda trilled, flicking her tail with glee. 'This could be the big break I've been waiting for my whole life.' She smiled dreamily, and then added, 'I'm sure there'll be roles for the rest of you too.'

'Not for me,' Danny the Faun sighed. 'I'm just queuing for support. They already have an award-winning director—the magnificent Trevor Phatt-Bunns—but it's a great opportunity for you, Miranda.'

'I'm still not sure I've picked the right scene for my audition,' Miranda said. 'I'd have made a lovely, if soggy, Juliet from *Romeo and Juliet*. Or perhaps I should have chosen the dying swan scene from Swan Lake?' Miranda paused and then sang, '♫ Qua-a-a-a-ck! Aaaargh ♫'

'Dur! Fish for brains!' heckled Arnie the Unicorn, who'd managed to get a spot ahead of us in the queue and kept reminding us about it. 'Swans don't quack.'

'Don't they?' Miranda asked us.

We shook our heads.

'Maybe they do when they're dying,' Miranda yelled at Arnie. 'Don't be judgey.'

'Whatever,' Arnie harrumphed, with a toss of his tail. 'Mermaids are so stupid.'

'Tell that to the producers of this *mermaid show*,' Miranda retorted. 'You big bully.'

'Ignore him, Miranda. You'd make a lovely dead swan,' Danny reassured her. 'But as they're looking for a mermaid and you *are* a mermaid, it makes sense to do a scene with a mermaid in it.'

'I should have chosen the scene from *Peter Pan* where the mermaids try to drown Wendy,' Miranda replied. 'With Arnie playing Wendy.'

'Miranda!' I protested. 'You can't drown Arnie. He's my friend and fellow unicorn.'

'I wouldn't really hurt him. Well, not much.' Miranda sighed at my expression. 'OK, OK, no messing with Arnie. Bo-o-oring.'

'Stop worrying about your audition,' Danny told her. 'Ariel from The Little Mermaid is the perfect choice.'

'Of course it is!' I cheered. 'I make a fabulous Sebastian the Crab. Check out my funky plastic crab claws.'

'Louie!' Danny narrowed his eyes at

me. 'Remember what we agreed? This is Miranda's audition.'

'It's OK,' Miranda said. 'I want my friends involved. Louie IS a fabulous Sebastian. And Frank . . . well . . . Frank would make a fantastic King Triton.' She beamed up at him and sang, '♪♩ So big, so powerful, so . . . ♩'

'I don't want to be Triton!' Frank growled. 'I want to be Flounder the Fish.'

'Yes, we know!'

We giggled as we looked at Frank. Despite being two metres tall and two metres wide, he had squeezed his wide warty face and hairy troll body into a tiny yellow and blue fish costume. Even in a queue of crazily dramatic auditionees, a troll dressed as a fish

was attracting attention—in particular, as he was accompanied by a fawn, a mermaid in a tank on wheels, and a unicorn wearing crab claws.

'You make a lovely Flounder, Frank,' Miranda assured him with a giggle. 'Come on, let's practise our group audition. ♫ **We'll knock their socks off.** ♫'

I jumped up and down. 'We are having ALL the fun. Can you believe I found such realistic pincers at such short notice?'

'YES, I CAN!' Frank yelled. 'Because you keep pinching my bottom with them. And that will stop being funny very quickly now we're stuck in the longest queue in history.'

Chapter Two

Buffalo Bob

Frank wasn't exaggerating about the length of the queue. Well, not much. People had come from all over the world to audition, and they were trying all sorts of tricks to get into the theatre ahead of the rest of us.

Girls in tutus said they felt faint and needed to get inside to cool down, only to recover miraculously when offered a lift home. Boys in tap shoes claimed to be on guest lists that didn't exist. And angry mothers insisted they had friends waiting for their children inside—except they couldn't remember their names.

The bouncers were having none of it, and everyone who tried to push in got sent straight to the back of the queue. 'No special cases,' they insisted.

'That's a good thing,' Frank said. 'But we're still never going to get in. There are thousands in front of us.'

I pinched him with a crab claw again, for being negative, but he had a point. The only thing moving in this queue was a strange, shouty man wearing a Stetson hat, a gold leather necktie, and a pair of

shiny cowboy boots, who wandered up and down the line, stopping every now and again to peer at anyone who caught his eye. His grin was as shiny as his boots.

He stopped in front of us and clapped his hands when he saw Miranda. 'Magnificent costume! I can hardly see where the tail's attached. You'd almost pass for a genuine mermaid!'

'♫ I AM a genuine mermaid ♫,' Miranda protested.

'That voice! She sings too!' The man rocked back on his cowboy-boot heels and whistled. 'You're going to be a huge star, little lady. Just follow me and let Buffalo Bob Parker be the brains behind your success.' He strode towards the front of the queue, pulling Miranda behind him.

'My friends too?' Miranda asked.

'As you wish, baby. With me as your manager, your every wish will be granted.'

' "Baby"?' I stared at Miranda. She didn't look like any baby I'd ever seen.

'♫ **"Manager"?** ♫ ' Miranda trilled, and when she looked at Buffalo Bob Parker, I could almost see the stars in her eyes.

'Wait,' Danny protested. 'If we move, we'll lose our place here. It's not a great spot but there are thousands of people behind us and the bouncers are sending everyone who tries to push in to the back of the queue.'

'You heard my cowboy manager,' Miranda said, giving Arnie a little wave as she passed him. '♫ I can have whatever I want. ♫'

'Yeah, baby,' I said with a giggle, prancing to the front with Miranda.

Danny sighed, but he and Frank followed along behind us.

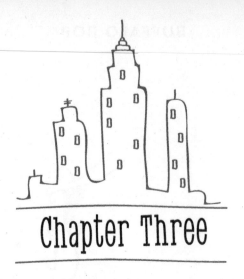

Chapter Three

A Real-life Mermaid

The bouncers glanced up grumpily. It was a long, hot afternoon. They were sweaty. And their sweat smelt of impatience with a hint of sulkiness.

Before we even reached them, one raised his arm, exposing a very sweaty armpit, and pointed to the back of the queue.

Buffalo Bob Parker grabbed the bouncer's

raised hand and shook it heartily. 'No need to thank me, young man. Just let us through.'

'No special treatment. Everyone waits in line. The Boss says so.'

Buffalo Bob Parker continued pumping the bouncer's hand. 'Can you imagine how impressed "the Boss" will be when you tell him you've found a REAL-LIFE MERMAID for his show?'

The bouncer used his free hand to push his sunglasses up, so he could study Miranda more closely.

'You're seriously telling me this is a genuine mermaid?' the bouncer asked, pulling his other arm free.

'♫ Ahem ♫,' Miranda coughed. 'I am

here, you know. And yes, genuine mermaid.'

'Prove it,' the Bouncer said.

'Just look at that divinely radiant tail,' Buffalo Bob said. 'Beautiful, magical . . .'

Miranda beamed at the compliments until Buffalo Bob added, 'Tug it. You'll see it's real.'

'♫ Oi! ♫,' Miranda protested as the bouncer reached towards her.

'I have an idea!' I blurted as Miranda prepared to wallop the bouncer with her "divinely radiant tail". 'Go underwater for five minutes, Miranda. No human could do that without coming up for air.'

'Er, actually they could,' Danny said. 'There's a Swedish man who can hold his breath underwater for over twenty minutes.'

'Impossible!' I turned to Miranda. 'Isn't it?'

'No idea. But if you want proof, watch this.' Miranda did an underwater somersault in her tank then emerged from the water and combed her perfect curls.

'It's dry!' The Bouncer stared in disbelief. 'Your hair's dry.'

'♪ **Mermaid magic** ♪,' Miranda sang.

'Convinced?' Buffalo Bob asked.

The Bouncer nodded, murmuring, 'A real-life mermaid. Wow! I can't wait to tell my old mum about this.' He waved Miranda through.

'What about us?' Frank bellowed.

The Bouncer looked at me, Frank, and Danny. He didn't seem quite as impressed. 'A horse with a shiny horn and crab claws, a big ogre thing, and a . . . what exactly are you?' He prodded Danny the Faun. 'Some sort of goat boy?'

'They're with me,' Miranda said. 'So if you want me then you have to let them in too.'

'Already issuing diva demands?' Danny

said, half laughing, half frowning.

'You heard my cowboy manager.' Miranda gave a toss of her magical mermaid hair and a harmonious warble. '♪ **What I want, I get, baby!** ♪'

Chapter Four

The Audition

We followed Miranda into the theatre, where people dressed in black whisked us up on to the stage.

'♫ Hello ♫,' Miranda sang. '♫ What can I perform for you today? ♫'

'Do you always sing everything?' asked a voice in the darkness.

'Not always.' Miranda tried to take the song out of her voice and failed.

'♪ Sorry. ♪'

'Don't be sorry. And don't stop!'

'♪ OK-A-A-Y ♪,' Miranda trilled. '♪ I am so excited to be here today. ♪' She paused and did a couple of somersaults in her tank. 'Getting this role would be my dream come true. How can I convince you I'm right for the part?'

'I think you already have. You can sing. You've got the tail, the hair, and you even come with your own tank. How can any actress—however great—make as good a mermaid as a real-life fishy female?'

'Um, I like what you're saying,' Miranda said carefully. 'But I'm going to object to the term "fishy female".'

'Apologies, Miranda the unfishy female.

You're in! Leave your details and we'll be in touch.'

'♪ Oooh. ♪' Miranda clapped her hands with glee. 'And my friends? Can they have

parts too?'

'I'm sure we can find a little something
for them to do.'

'Should we audition now?' Frank asked.

'No need,' said the voice in the dark.

We were ushered off the stage and back out into the street as Miranda stayed behind to fill in all the paperwork.

'Why no need?' Frank asked. 'They have to see what we can do to give us the right parts.'

'I am sure everything will work out swimmingly,' I said, grinning. 'See what I did there? That was a mermaid joke! Fear not, Frank, our *tail* will have a happy ending. Tail like a mermaid's tail. See what I—'

Frank grabbed me by my crab pincers. 'Yes, I see what you did there. Don't do it again.'

'Frank! You're hurting me on *porpoise*. Ha ha! Get it? Porpoise, like the sea creature? See what—?'

'GRRRR!' Frank was starting to look less like his normal cuddly self and more like the kind of troll who likes to eat unicorns for breakfast.

Luckily, that was when Miranda reappeared. Frank released my pincers and told her he was worried about the lack of auditions.

'♪ **Don't worry**. ♪ ' She patted him on the shoulder. 'They don't need you to audition. They only gave you the part because I asked them to.'

Frank went quiet after that.

Chapter Five

Miranda's Marvels

Splash it Up! was the talk of New York so the teachers at our School for Performing Arts were thrilled one of their pupils had the starring role. Obviously not as thrilled as Miranda, who looked ready to explode with excitement.

I was ecstatic for her, so I didn't mind my headmistress and favourite teacher, Madame Swirler, replacing the photos from our recent Interstate Dance Championship (including several very flattering pictures of me performing the Leaping Champion jump) with posters of Miranda.

I did mind a little bit when Miranda moved my 'special commendation' ballet certificate from the main hall noticeboard to the back of the toilet door so she could make room for newspaper clippings about her being the 'next big thing'. But I cheered up when Danny pointed out people spend far more time in the toilet than by the main noticeboard.

Arnie *definitely* minded Miranda moving his pictures. His response was to change the spelling of 'Miranda the Mermaid' to 'Miran-DUR the MEH-maid' on the *Splash it Up!* posters. (Don't tell Miranda, but I thought that was funny.)

Miranda didn't find it funny at all. She punished Arnie by offering to swap any of his fans' 'Arnie's Army' T-shirt for a brand-new 'Miranda's Marvels' T-shirt. Buffalo Bob, her cowboy manager, had created them and they were super shiny, with a special sparkly mermaid tail you could attach with Velcro at the back.

'ARGHnie is just jealous,' Miranda told the crowd that had started appearing everywhere she went when the huge billboard posters of her face popped up across the city. 'He must feel like a loser because the *Splash it Up!* team wouldn't even let him audition. Ha ha.'

The crowd of 'Miranda's Marvels' laughed. I didn't. They hadn't let me audition either.

And Frank and I still hadn't heard anything about our roles.

Meanwhile, Miranda had been sent a rehearsal schedule, so we crowded around it in the dorm.

'They want you almost every day!' I cheered. 'You're a big star now, Miranda. How will you fit in your lessons here?'

Miranda shrugged. 'I guess I'll learn on the job.'

'Wow!' I bounced. 'This is all sooooo exciting!'

Frank studied Miranda's schedule and burped with pleasure. 'Brilliant. Look! You're free for the whole day on my birthday! The four of us can do something fun.'

'♪ Can't think of anything I'd like more ♪,' trilled Miranda. 'I don't want my new role to change what we do as friends.'

'Why would it?' Danny asked.

'♪ No reason ♪,' Miranda sang breezily. 'You guys run on to class. I just need to call Buffalo Bob. You know, my *manager*, dahlings.'

Chapter Six

Rehearsals

Frank and I accompanied Miranda to the first rehearsal at the John Feelgood Theatre. I couldn't wait to find out what roles they'd given us.

The minute we arrived, everyone swooped on Miranda and tried to lift her onto their shoulders, chanting, 'the next big thing', like in the newspaper clippings. It all got a bit damp and slippery, like a group of people trying to hold on to a large, slithery fish. Frank caught Miranda as she whooshed between the hands of two lighting engineers towards the first row of seats. She gave him a grateful smile as he dropped her back into her tank and placed her on the stage.

I followed behind and addressed the theatre crew. 'Greetings. I am Louie the Unicorn and this is Frank the Troll. We wondered where you wanted us to stand?'

No one replied. Instead, they trampled Frank and me in their rush to get on stage and talk to Miranda.

It's hard to trample a troll so you can imagine how much they wanted to see her. The pre-show publicity had got everyone super-excited.

I told myself being ignored might be a good thing. Madame Swirler always said you shouldn't spoil talented people, because they won't realize they have to work for success if everyone acts like they've already made it.

So, maybe this was a good sign. No one was acting as if I'd already made it. No one was acting as if I even existed. They must *really* want me to succeed.

'Hello?' I tried again. 'Hello?'

Nothing. The rehearsal had begun and everyone was noisily cheering every note Miranda sang.

It was very different to Madame Swirler's shouty method of teaching. All the whistling and clapping certainly made Miranda smile more, but Madame Swirler's snapping and criticism did make you try harder.

Anyway, no need for *me* to worry about it. No one was clapping and cheering me. When Frank finally managed to make himself heard to ask what we were supposed to be doing, he was told they'd figure out what to do with us later, if it made Miranda happy.

Frank picked his nose, which was usually a sign he'd forgotten he was calmer and lovelier than the average troll.

I tried to cheer him up. 'That's good news, Frank. It *will* make Miranda happy if they give us roles. So they *will* figure out what to do with us.'

That didn't help. Frank just moved his warty finger from his nose to his mouth. Ewww. I moved away and watched Miranda prepare for stardom.

She had a wonderful voice and got the songs right quickly. She wasn't so comfortable with the talky bits, maybe because the words of the play were a little strange. They were all about being pretty and popular, and I was surprised they thought that was enough to take the business world by storm in the way the audition poster described.

But Miranda was clearly enjoying herself. As a uniquely dashing actor myself, I was proud of the unusual approach she was taking to the craft.

Sadly, those of us with original acting skills are doomed to be mocked by those who don't understand. A couple behind us sniggered every time Miranda spoke, and muttered things like, 'That mermaid sings like an angel, but couldn't

act her way out of a puddle—wearing a rubber ring.'

When they went quiet, I assumed they'd been won over by the power of Miranda's acting. But when I turned around, I saw that Frank had his hands over their mouths.

I squeaked and tugged his arms away. It was right to support Miranda—she was our friend and no one should mock her—but Frank couldn't just stop people breathing! The girl critic's face had turned slightly blue and the boy's throw-uppy expression suggested Frank's troll hands might still be covered in bogies.

When Frank released them, they fled backstage to the dressing rooms. I know because I saw them there later when we went to find Miranda during her break. Luckily, Frank didn't spot them as they ducked behind a large bouquet of roses when they saw him coming.

We found Miranda talking to the director. Frank had sent her a note earlier asking her to speak to him about our roles.

Miranda's manager, Buffalo Bob, was sitting with them, and as we approached I heard him mutter, 'Ditch the flying horse and the ogre, baby. They're dragging you down.'

'Oooh! Did you hear that?' I poked Frank. 'Maybe those guys will want to be friends.'

Frank kicked a costume rail and sent twenty sparkly tutus shooting across the room.

'Frank!' I said. 'Stop kicking and start listening. Miranda's manager says there's a flying horse and an ogre here. They might want to hang out with us.'

'There's no flying horse, Louie. And you're looking at the ogre. That horrible man couldn't even be bothered to get our species right.'

'I don't understand.'

'No, I don't suppose you do.' Frank patted my shoulder. 'Life is probably nicer that way.' He paused by a bowl of blue M&Ms, ate a handful, and then threw the rest at Buffalo Bob, who ducked and glowered at us.

Chapter Seven

Frank's Birthday

I was so excited about Frank's birthday. Our friend Victoria Sponge at the Sunshine Sparkle-Dust Café had made a giant cake with pictures of Frank, Danny, Miranda, and me on the top, and Frank had promised we could all eat ourselves later!

But first we were going to do a mini birthday show to celebrate how FUNTASTIC our lives had been since we left Story Land and arrived in New York in search of adventure. Our first performance together had been in the Sunshine Sparkle-Dust Café, and I was looking forward to reliving our famous conga-through-the-cupcakes there later.

After that, Frank and I planned to do a repeat performance of our starring roles as the Handsome Prince (me) and the Scary Giant (Frank) in the rescue scene from *The Handsome Prince and the Princess Pointlessly Stuck in the Tower* we'd performed on Broadway, two terms ago.

Miranda pointed out, several times, that had been a one-off school performance, not a 'proper show' like *Splash it Up!* But we'd still been the talk of the city . . . OK, the talk of a little bit of the city . . . OK, OK, the talk of Frank and me. But we lived in the city, so that still counted. Whatever! It was going to be brilliant to do our favourite scene all over again.

To finish the show, each of us planned to do our own special number. For me that would be my Leaping Champion jump from the interstate dance championship. After all, it was worthy of a 'special commendation', as anyone who'd been to the toilet recently, and seen my certificate on the back of the door, would know.

The main thing was we'd all be together. FRIENDSHIP WAS FUN, and we had a whole day to celebrate it. We hadn't seen enough of Miranda lately. Even when she was with us she was busy signing autographs and shaking hands, so we didn't have time to talk.

But she'd be all ours today. We'd been talking about Frank's birthday for weeks and none of us would dream of missing it. I couldn't wait!

I was still smiling when I entered the dorm room. My grin faded slightly when I found Miranda ordering Frank to give her a manicure and Danny to clean the inside of her tank.

'♪ **Louie!** ♪' she sang. 'Thank goodness you're here.'

I beamed. She'd obviously missed me as much as I'd missed her.

'You're just in time to scrub my tail.'

'Hmm,' I murmured. 'Perhaps another time. I've got my special rainbow-tastic disco outfit on, ready for Frank's birthday celebrations. I don't think I'm supposed to get the flashing lights and sequins wet.'

Miranda scowled as her new mobile phone buzzed. She pulled her hand away from Frank's to answer the call, smudging the nail varnish he'd been carefully applying.

She giggled into the receiver, tossing her hair as she sang, '♫ **Who, me? Yes, me! Oh yes, I am rather wonderful.** ♫ '

She finished the conversation with, 'Yes! Oh yes! Of course I will. I'd love to.'

She dropped the phone back into its waterproof bag and waved at Frank.

'Frank, dahling. Take me down to reception.'

'Please!' Danny reminded her.

'Please what, Danny?' she asked. 'Ah, you want to continue cleaning my tank? Of course you can, sweetie. *Mwah, mwah.* You'll just have to wait until later.'

'No,' Danny replied. 'I don't particularly want to clean your tank, Miranda. What I meant was, you should say "please" to Frank, rather than giving him orders.'

'Frank doesn't mind, do you, dahling? It's his birthday, so I'm letting him treat me.' Miranda gave Frank a little tickle under his chin, which made him sneeze. Miranda withdrew her hand quickly. Troll snot is not a pretty thing.

'I'm not sure whether I mind or not yet,' Frank replied, wiping his nose on his sleeve. 'Who was that on the phone, Miranda? And what would you love to do?'

Miranda blushed. 'It's nothing, really, Frank. It was just Buffalo Bob. My cowboy manager,' she added unnecessarily.

'We know who he is,' Frank said with a giant snort. 'What does he want you to do? ON MY BIRTHDAY?!'

'Only a teeny little meeting, sweetie. Won't take a second. It's just . . . the film star Andromeda Jolene is in New York and Buffalo Bob thinks it might be nice for me to spend some time with her, and of course be *totally* surprised when the paparazzi turn up.'

'It might also be nice for you to spend some time with us,' Frank growled. 'ON MY BIRTHDAY.'

'Of course, sweetie, I'll be with you on your birthday. ♫ **Happy Birthday to yoooooooooou**. ♫ But it's not all day, is it?'

'Well, yes,' Danny pointed out. 'That's the point of birthdays. They are all day, aren't they? Birth-day. All-day. Plus, Frank has spent ages making sure today will be perfect.'

'I know, sweetie, dahling—*mwah*— but you wouldn't want me to miss the opportunity to meet Andromeda, would you?'

Frank and Danny's faces suggested they definitely would like her to miss that opportunity. But I understood why Miranda was excited. Andromeda Jolene could find lost treasure in tombs, perform incredible feats of kung fu as a tigress, and fly—at least she could until they chopped her wings off. Hmm. On reflection, perhaps she could only do these things in films. But it would still be thrilling to meet her.

'Why don't we wave Miranda on her way to meet this super-famous lady?' I suggested. 'I'm sure she won't be more than a few minutes. We've all been looking forward to your party for weeks, Frank, and Miranda would obviously rather be with us.'

Miranda nodded, although I noticed she kept glancing at her phone.

'She can meet us at Sunshine Sparkle-Dust Café for the show, in an hour. We're going to have so much fun together.'

A horn beeped below. I looked out of the window and saw Buffalo Bob Parker peering up from a truck that had 'Miranda the Magnificent Mermaid' painted on the side.

'Looks like your lift is here.'

'♫ **Door, dahling** ♫,' Miranda trilled at Frank, who just stared at her. Miranda stopped preening for a moment and looked more like her old self. 'Please, Frank, would you mind helping me into my transport?'

He grunted, but did as she asked. I

heard her telling him not to worry, she'd be back in plenty of time for the show, dahling.

Five hours later, Frank and I were doing our final bows on the café counter-slash-stage and thanking Danny for his brilliant direction. The huge crowd in the café cheered, but I heard lots of them mumbling things like, 'I thought Miranda the famous mermaid would be here. That's the only reason I came.'

I know Frank heard them too because he scratched his armpits and forgot to say 'Pardon me' after a bottom burp. But he was pretending it didn't matter.

He kept up his slightly scary birthday

smile until everyone else had gone and the three of us were sitting around the counter enjoying the super-delicious birthday cake. Frank ate fondant Frank. Danny gobbled up fondant Danny. And I devoured fondant Louie. Mmm. Only a quarter of the cake remained. The quarter of the cake with Miranda on it.

A fly landed on her beautifully iced face.

None of us brushed it away.

Chapter Eight

Getting our Skates on

The atmosphere in our dorm was sticky after Frank's birthday, and not just because we forgot to wash our hands and hooves after eating all that cake. Everyone was still upset about Miranda's disappearance on Frank's birthday and about the fact she'd told Frank and me— BY TEXT—there were no longer roles for us in the *Splash it Up!* show.

Danny ordered Miranda to apologize to Frank. She did, but she didn't sound at all sorry: she sounded more like she was cross with us for bothering her with such trivia when she was so busy and important.

We hardly saw her any more. It made me sad and left a Miranda-sized hole in my life. And that was a big hole. A mermaid-in-a-tank-sized hole.

I never stopped trying to include her in everything we did—inviting her to parties and school events and trips to the shops or the café, but she was always busy.

Finally, though, I thought of something fun to do on one of Miranda's rare free evenings. Go to a roller disco! We had always talked about going to one of those together, so I spent all week in the school's prop department making a special pair of flashing roller wheels to stick on the bottom of her tank and a glitter ball to hang inside it.

Miranda said she was grateful, but gave a large yawn. 'I don't think I'll be able to make it, Louie. I'm sooooo tired. It's all "schedule this", "rehearsal that". I need a rest.'

I felt disappointed, but I understood. She'd been working so hard, no wonder she just wanted a quiet night in bed.

Before we left for the roller disco I set up the glitter ball on the dorm ceiling, decorated the room with fairy lights, and

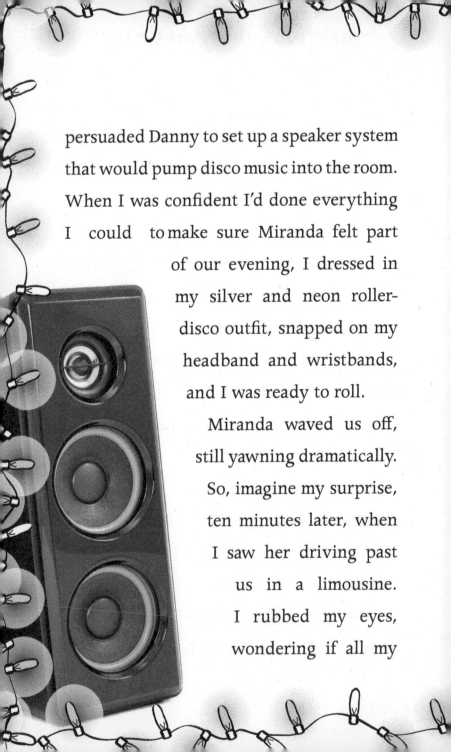

persuaded Danny to set up a speaker system that would pump disco music into the room. When I was confident I'd done everything I could to make sure Miranda felt part of our evening, I dressed in my silver and neon roller-disco outfit, snapped on my headband and wristbands, and I was ready to roll.

Miranda waved us off, still yawning dramatically. So, imagine my surprise, ten minutes later, when I saw her driving past us in a limousine. I rubbed my eyes, wondering if all my hard work in the dorm was making me hallucinate.

I looked again.

No. There was no mistake. The limousine had been customized to allow her tank to stick out of the top so her hair could blow in the breeze. Buffalo Bob sat alongside her and they were both drinking pink fizzy stuff, their heads thrown back with laughter.

I turned indignantly to tell Danny and Frank.

But I stopped when I saw how happy they looked, chatting about the moves we were going to make at tonight's roller disco. I didn't want to upset them with my disturbing news.

My horn twitched uneasily as I realized that, not only was Miranda lying to me; she was also stopping me telling the truth to my best friends.

This had to stop. This was not the unicorn way.

Chapter Nine

Moving on

The roller disco was a fun-filled extravaganza of sparkling lights, shiny costumes, and killer dance moves, but I couldn't stop thinking about Miranda's betrayal, all evening. I tried to talk to her the following morning, but she wouldn't listen.

'You're killing my buzz, Louie. I expected you of all people to be more supportive.'

'Buzz?' I asked in confusion. 'Are you learning to talk to insects? Cool! I bet bees are fun to chat to.'

'Don't be silly, dahling. It's something Buffalo Bob told me . . .' She smiled when she mentioned his name and it made me want to poke him with my horn. ' "Killing your buzz" is what people do when you become famous, because they're jealous. People tell me my acting sucks because it's so great. They want to be me, but they can't, so they try to kill my buzz.'

'Huh? So when people say your acting is bad, what they actually mean is it's super-spectacularly good?'

Miranda nodded.

This put a new spin on our Madame

Swirler's comments in dance lessons. I must be the most amazing student that ever lived. Nice!

One thing still confused me. 'How am *I* killing your buzz?'

'By saying it was wrong of me to go out on the night of the roller disco.'

'But it *was* wrong of you.' I was finding this conversation confusing. 'So if I'm telling the truth about this, maybe Madame Swirler is telling the truth when she says I need to do more practice and maybe the people who say your acting is bad are . . . Oh.'

I stopped when I saw the look on Miranda's face, but it was too late. In her head I'd already said it.

'You think I can't act,' she wailed.

'No. I don't think that. I didn't say that. I didn't even *nearly* say that. What I *nearly* said was other people might think you can't act. But I didn't mean it. I didn't even *nearly* mean it.'

Miranda wasn't listening. 'Buffalo Bob is right. You're all jealous. I shouldn't listen to anyone.'

'You can't ignore everyone. What about your director? The acting coaches?'

'Negative, negative, negative,' Miranda waved her hand dismissively. 'Laters, haters.'

'I'm not a hater. I'm your best friend.'

Miranda covered her ears with her hands. 'Not listening. ♫ **La la la**. ♫ My

cowboy manager is right. I don't belong here any more. I need to move onwards and upwards. I need support. I need positivity. I need to feel the ♫ **la-la-looove**. ♫ '

'But that's what you get from us.' I said. 'Well, the stuff at the beginning. I don't know about all this la-la-looove business.'

'He says you bring me down and he's right,' Miranda continued. 'You tell me off for having fun. You tell me I can't act.' She ignored my protests. 'Well, my *manager* has found me the perfect flat, right next to the theatre. He says I need space to be creative, to express myself, to prepare for my big role.'

With that, she flung open the dorm room door and ordered the group of Miranda's Marvels waiting outside to pack her stuff up so she could leave for her new life.

I didn't want things to end on such a bad note, so I told Miranda to come back in an hour after I'd made sure the speakers and the glitter ball were still working and I'd put my neon outfit back on. Then we could have a lovely big leaving party and send her off with a bang.

She did go out with a bang.

The bang of Danny and Frank slamming the dormitory door. Because Miranda didn't even bother to turn up.

'I'm sure she's very busy,' I said quietly.

'Enough is enough, Louie,' Danny told me. 'She can't even be bothered to come to a party you've organized in her honour. That has to tell you something. I've had enough of that mermaid. I'm not going to her silly *Splash it Up!* show. Especially now you and Frank aren't even in it. Besides, have you seen the price of the tickets?'

'Yes, but don't worry, Danny. Arnie says the main actors get three free tickets. I'm sure Miranda will give hers to us.'

'I'll believe it when I see it,' Danny growled.

Chapter Ten

Tickets

Miranda must have had a good reason for not giving us her free tickets. I'd just have to find another way to get some. Friendship was friendship and she had always been there for all of my performances. The problem was how to get the money for a ticket?

Fortunately, Victoria Sponge had a solution.

'This is perfect timing,' she said, wiping icing sugar from her cheeks. 'We're having a huge promotional doughnut-eating contest here at the Sunshine Sparkle-Dust Café next week and I've always said that horn of yours is the perfect doughnut-hole-punch. If you're happy to help me out by horn-punching holes in doughnuts, I can give you the money for a ticket. Tickets for doughnuts. Win-win.'

The only challenge left was persuading Danny and Frank to buy tickets too.

'I know you're angry,' I said, 'But we're best friends and best friends support each other no matter how silly the other best friend is being.' I opened the box of chocolate-filled, chocolate-sprinkled

doughnuts Victoria Sponge had given me earlier as a thank you for agreeing to help her out with the contest. 'Plus, if you buy a ticket, I'll give you a doughnut.'

'No, Louie,' Danny said. 'If Miranda had wanted us to be there, she'd have sent tickets.' He made a gesture at Frank that I didn't understand until they both dived on my doughnuts and started stuffing their faces. 'Besides, best friends support each other *with doughnuts*, no matter what!'

I tried to protest, but I got the giggles and grabbed a handful of doughnuts for myself. 'So,' I mumbled through a mouthful of chocolate fondant and chocolate sprinkles, 'are you saying you'd come if Miranda sent tickets?'

' 'Spose so,' Danny muttered.

'What if I could get tickets from somewhere else?'

Frank scratched his armpit thoughtfully, but Danny was firm. 'No. If Miranda doesn't invite us, we're not going.'

Bah! I knew they wanted to go. But now Danny had made a big deal about it, there was no shifting them, and it didn't look like Miranda was going to send tickets any time soon.

I tried talking to Arnie about it. He yawned. 'Boring. Just buy the stupid tickets and pretend Miranda sent them.'

'Lie?' I whinnied in horror. 'I can't lie! That is not the unicorn way.'

Arnie harrumphed scornfully. 'Did your

father ever ask your mother if his bottom looked big with a newly fashioned tail style?'

I nodded.

'And what did she say?'

'She always said his bottom looked lovely.'

'But did it sometimes look big behind his tail?'

I didn't answer.

'There you go. You're always telling me your mother is the most wonderful unicorn in Story Land. Well, she says you should lie to your friends.'

'Um. No she doesn't. *You* say I should lie to them.'

'Whatever. I have given you a solution.

It's up to you whether you use it.'

Much as I loved Arnie, I'd learned over time it wasn't always wise to follow his advice, so I checked with Victoria Sponge.

'I can certainly give you enough work to pay for three tickets,' she said. 'We're very busy this week because of the contest, so that's not a problem.'

'But is Arnie right? Should I lie to my friends?'

'I have an idea.' Victoria Sponge pulled up a chair and handed me a brownie. 'Sit down, hear me out and see what you think.'

Two days later I raced up to the dorm room, ignoring Miranda's empty bed.

'She sent them!' I cheered. 'The tickets

are here! We're going to *Splash it Up!'*

'Miranda sent us tickets!' Frank grinned, reaching for them.

I followed Victoria Sponge's advice and didn't explain that 'she' was in fact the ticket lady from the kiosk where I'd bought the tickets.

'Really?' Danny emerged from the bathroom, toothpaste still on his chin.

I let Frank answer for me. 'Yes, Danny,' he said. 'Look! Here! Three tickets for the show. Isn't that amazing?'

'AMAZING, ASTOUNDING, MARVELLOUS, AND MIRACULOUS!

You are coming, right?' I checked, wincing as I spoke. My horn still ached from several late-night sessions of doughnut-punching.

'Guess so,' Danny said, trying not to look too pleased about it, but I could tell he was thrilled.

Chapter Eleven

The Performance

There was an excited murmur as everyone took their seats for the opening night of *Splash it Up!* The queue to get in had been almost as long as the audition queue on that hot afternoon all those weeks ago.

The curtain rose, revealing Miranda surrounded by a crowd of briefcase-wielding, suit-wearing business people in front of a huge backdrop of the Manhattan skyline. People were still gossiping amongst themselves. No critics had written any advance reviews for the show and people were wondering why. It usually meant a show wasn't good, but that was obviously impossible with all these famous producers and composers and directors involved.

Except it wasn't impossible.

As the show went on, the audience fell silent apart from embarrassed giggles, a few 'blimeys', and some unkind booing and hissing. The script was very strange— all about how brilliant and beautiful the mermaid was, and nothing else. And while Miranda's singing *was* beautiful, people didn't seem to 'get' her acting.

An entire row got up and left after twenty minutes and lots of people followed shortly after. Hardly anyone came back after the interval and by the end of the show Frank, Danny, and I were three of only about twenty people left in the theatre.

We tried to talk to Miranda afterwards, but she ran away, and we couldn't find her no matter how hard we looked.

THE DAILY DOUGHNUT

Mermaid Tanks!

SHOWBIZ ON SUNDAY

LITTLE (TALENT) MERMAID

The following morning, the newspapers ran with nasty headlines:

THE FAIRY TALE TIMES

MAID TO FAIL

SHOWBIZ NEWS

SPLASH IT UP! A WASHOUT

THE GOLDEN GLOBE

FISH FARCE BATTERED

THE DAILY NEWS

Mermaid Tanks!

During the week, we all tried to get hold of Miranda. We tried phoning, we tried texting, we tried emailing, someone even suggested sending a pigeon. I think they were joking, but you can never tell. However, Miranda refused to speak to anyone.

By the weekend, the big announcement was:

The reviews had been so critical and the audiences so small that they decided to close the show after just two weeks.

We went around to Miranda's new apartment block and tried shouting up at her room but she wouldn't come to the window. We tried sneaking in, but it was full of actors and actresses managed by Miranda's cowboy manager, Buffalo Bob, and they weren't very nice to us.

To be honest, they weren't very nice to anyone. No one said thank you to the pizza delivery man who came while we were there, and we watched in shock as a group of dancers let the door slam on a plumber. They didn't even apologize when it made him drop his toolbox on his toe.

'They don't even look at these people,' Danny said. 'It's like they're not there.'

I felt my horn tingle. 'That's it! That's

how I can get into the building! If I dress up as some kind of tradesperson they won't even look at me. It will be easy to get in.'

Frank and Danny clapped. I bowed happily. I deserved the applause. It *was* a good idea.

We returned to school and raided the costume closet. I emerged in a vest and dungarees with a cap balanced on my horn and a tool belt around my waist.

'WHAT DO YOU THREE THINK YOU'RE DOING?' Madame Swirler appeared out of nowhere. How did she always know when you were doing something wrong?

'HOW DARE YOU MESS ABOUT

WITH MY COSTUMES?'

I lowered my horn in shame. Unicorns do not sneak around. (We generally prance.)

Frank and Danny were less embarrassed.

'It's a rescue mission,' Danny declared. 'Louie is going to sneak in and save Miranda, dressed as a handyman.'

I waited for Madame Swirler to yell something like, 'Off with the unicorn's head.'

She didn't. Instead she said, 'Wait here.' She ducked into the prop cupboard and came out brandishing a large spanner. 'Here. Your costume is now complete. Go get her, Tiger.'

'Thank you. But I think you're confused, Madame Swirler. I'm a unicorn, not a tiger. You may have been tricked by my disguise.' I lifted my cap. ' 'Tis I, Louie.'

Madame Swirler raised the spanner over my head and for a moment I thought she was going to wallop me with it. But she just growled and handed it to me as she shoved me out the door. 'Might be best not to speak on this mission, Louie. Just hurry up and bring Miranda back where she belongs.'

Chapter Twelve

Breaking In

The costume worked perfectly. None of the divas in Miranda's apartment block paid any attention to a lowly handyman—not even one with a horn—so I made it through the main entrance and up the stairs with no difficulty. The problem came when I arrived at Miranda's door. I could hear splashes inside but she refused to answer.

'Open up,' I ordered. 'I am a handyman and many things in your apartment need, um, handy-ing.'

Nothing.

'I have a spanner.'

Still nothing

'It's a really big spanner.'

Silence.

Hmm. Honesty might be the best policy.

'OK, I'm not a handyman,' I confessed. 'Shh, don't tell anyone, but it's me, Louie. Please let me in, Miranda.' I heard movement and guessed she'd come to peer through the spyhole.

Still no answer.

I remembered my disguise and lifted off the cap. ' 'Tis I, Louie.' Then, just in case

I still wasn't recognizable, I added, 'Louie the Unicorn.'

Still no answer.

I couldn't give up now. Not after we'd been to all this trouble. Madame Swirler was expecting me to succeed. No way was I going to let one apartment door stop me. I bashed it with my spanner. It didn't budge but the spanner squished slightly. Stupid fake tools! I shuddered at the thought of telling Madame Swirler I'd damaged one of her props. No more spanner-bashing.

What next?

Kick the door down?

Maybe my back legs were stronger than my front ones? It was worth a try. I did a handstand on Miranda's doormat and kicked as hard as I could. I thought I felt something move, but it must have been something inside me, as the door stayed stubbornly shut.

To make it worse, a group of performers I recognized from *Splash it Up!* came dancing up the stairs just as my hat fell off! What if they realized who I was and made me leave?

I dropped down onto my back legs, quickly placed the cap back on my head, and nodded at them in a handyman kind of way. 'Greetings, dramatic people. I am just a humble handyman. Pay no attention to me while I make sure all the doors are working properly. Carry on up the stairs. Nothing to see here. Definitely no unicorns.'

They giggled into their hands, but kept walking up to the next floor.

I glared at Miranda's door. I wouldn't be able to force my way through it without resorting to desperate measures.

'Come on, Miranda. Please let me in. Don't make me do something I'll regret.'

I'd heard that phrase on television and it usually worked. I hoped it would be enough to convince Miranda to open up.

It wasn't. The time had come for the horn of last resort.

'Step away from the entrance, Miranda,' I whinnied as I took a run-up and leapt at her apartment door.

My horn was magical. It could get through anything. And it did. It pierced the heavy apartment door with no trouble at all. The problem was the rest of me, which was stuck on the other side, dangling in the air.

'Um? Miranda? A little help?'

I heard a heavy sigh and finally the sound

of a key turning in the lock. I entered the room swinging around in a horn-stuck-in-the-door sort of way.

'Louie, what are you doing? Can't you take a hint? I don't want to see anyone. And I certainly don't need a new unicorn-shaped door knocker.'

'Perhaps you could, um, help me down?'

Miranda moved across and let me rest on her tank while I loosened my horn.

'Anyway, where was I? Oh yes, we miss you and we want you to come home.'

'Home?' Miranda sniffed.

'Yes,' I said as I slid off her tank. 'You belong at school. Madame Swirler says so. It'll always be your home.'

Miranda wouldn't look at me and the music had vanished from her voice. 'What if I don't want it to be?'

'I know you're a big star now, with your

name on posters and everything—' I pointed at the promotional pictures on Miranda's apartment walls '—but it's always nice to have friends.'

Tears started to trickle down Miranda's face and as I looked closer I saw she'd drawn little moustaches and pointy ears on her pictures.

'I'm not a star, Louie. I'm a laughing stock. A wet, fishy laughing stock.'

'You're a star to us, Miranda. You always will be. You have a beautiful, twinkly voice and you are a lovely twinkly person. Well, most of the time. Now, what about making yourself into a shooting star and whooshing back to school?'

Miranda reached out of her tank and

flung her arms around me. 'I'd love to, Louie. If you really mean it.' We stayed like that for a while. I wasn't sure whether the water trickling down my neck was from Miranda's tears or her tank. Eventually she pulled away. 'But you're always lovely, Louie, and you forgive everyone—you've had all that practice with Arnie! Everyone else must hate me.'

'Don't be silly,' I said. 'They'll probably have a whinge and a moan—I wouldn't mind a chat about moving certificates to toilets at some point—but best friends forever is best friends forever.' I pulled up her apartment window and waved at the two figures below. 'Frank! Danny! Up here! Miranda is coming home.'

Frank whooped and hollered and roared with glee and Danny looked quietly pleased. I buzzed them both into Miranda's apartment.

'What about Buffalo Bob?' Danny asked, pushing up his sleeves and looking around as if he expected to find Buffalo Bob lurking in a cupboard. 'Do we have to fight him?'

'He's gone,' Miranda said sadly. 'Along with the limousine and the flowers and his promises of whatever I wanted. Buffalo Bob says he doesn't do losers.'

'We'll show him who the loser is,' Frank growled, picking up Miranda's tank as if it weighed nothing and skipping all the way down two flights of stairs.

Chapter Thirteen

The Finale

Back at school, Miranda was quieter than normal, but we slowly slipped back into our old routines and the song slowly slipped back into her voice. However, her face always fell when the car came to pick her up for that night's show.

'Just try to enjoy it.' I told her. 'Don't let the critics kill your buzz.'

'Ha. Thanks for your support, Louie!'

Miranda smiled. 'Seriously! And not just now. Always. Victoria Sponge told me how hard you worked to get the tickets for the first night's show and I feel terrible. I could have got you free tickets. But I didn't know. Buffalo Bob took my tickets and sold them.'

'I knew you'd have sent them if you could!' I punched the air triumphantly, then whispered, 'Don't mention this to Frank and Danny. I tricked them and I feel bad about it—unicorns aren't supposed to lie.'

'Idiot!' Frank appeared behind me with a loud *BURRRRP*. 'We already figured it out and we're grateful, not cross.'

'Yeah,' Danny agreed. 'You wouldn't have had to lie if I hadn't been an idiot.'

'You're all idiots,' Miranda agreed with a grin. 'But you're my idiots. And I have free tickets for the final show . . . Not just three this time. LOADS! . . . I guess there are some advantages to no one wanting to see the show,' she said sadly, her grin disappearing. 'Anyway, I'd love it if you came. It would mean a lot to have my friends in the audience. Actually, it would mean a lot to have *anyone* in the audience.'

'We'll be there!'

The queues were shorter than they had been for the opening night, but there were still quite a few people in the theatre for the last night of *Splash it Up!*

Listening to them talk, as we waited to

take our seats, it seemed most of them had come just to see how bad it could really be.

'I hear it's a disaster. Most of the original cast have refused to perform.'

'Oh, that poor creature. Looks like she mer-made a terrible decision when she took this role. Ha ha.'

'Not funny,' I muttered under my breath. Poor Miranda. It must be hard to turn up every night to crowds like this. I had to help her.

So I cheered at the top of my voice when she came on stage, and then cheered louder and louder with every song that she sang.

At first Danny told me to shush, but when people started grumbling about how awful the show was and walking out of the theatre, he took a deep breath and joined in. So did Frank, and Frank was LOUD.

Before long, Frank, Danny, and I were leaping up and dancing around every time Miranda did anything.

A small group of children behind us joined in, and by the time Miranda began her 'Singing in the Drain' number, there

were at least fifty of us on our feet, singing along as best we could.

Miranda waved across at us and ignored the tuts and the frowns. It was time for the final song, but she paused before it.

'♫ **Hello, final night's audience!** ♫' she trilled. 'I want to dedicate this last number to my friends,' Miranda declared. 'They supported me when I was on the way up, even when I didn't have time for them. And they are still supporting me— ♫ **loudly** ♫ —on the way back down. It's when things go wrong that you can really tell who your friends are. So this song is for you, Louie, Danny, and Frank—"I Want to Hold Your Hand". Or hoof. Or, er, hairy knobbly thing with claws.'

The orchestra began and Miranda burst into song. After looking at each other uncertainly, the other actors on stage started to slowly join in. After a few lines, they were all involved and looked like they were having fun for the first time in the entire performance.

Miranda gestured for us to come up and join her on stage.

Danny ummed and ahed and stood up and sat down. I laughed and clambered over the top of him to canter down the aisle. I'd never say no to a chance to be on a Broadway stage. I beckoned to Frank who jumped to his feet, flung Danny over his shoulder, and joined me.

The audience weren't quite sure how to

react. A lot of people had already left and more were heading for the exits, but our fifty or so new friends were on their feet clapping and cheering and so were others dotted around the theatre.

There was also a big group at the front throwing things at us.

'Aww, look,' I said. 'They love us.'

'Um. Louie,' Danny snorted. 'That's not love. That's what is known as "unfriendly fire".'

'Pah! Nonsense. You're such a gloomburger, Danny. When people like you, they throw flowers and teddy bears on to the stage,' I explained.

'Yes. But this lot are throwing tomatoes.

And eggs.'

'And rocks. Ow!' yelled Frank as one bounced off his head.

'I'm sure they mean well,' I said, ducking to avoid a particularly squishy

looking tomato. 'Wait a minute!' I peered at the group, who'd paused to collect more ammunition. Some of them looked familiar. 'No way! It's Arnie's Army!'

And sitting right in the middle wearing a very large hat and dark glasses . . .

'ARNIE!' I yelled in delight, thrilled to see that he'd come after all. 'How marvellous!' I held out a leg towards him and sang, 'I want to hold your hoooooooof.'

Arnie sank down into his seat, and tipped his hat further over his eyes, obviously

overcome with joy.

'Join us, Arnie,' I cried, reaching out for him.

He seemed to be struggling to get up, but fortunately our fifty new friends danced down the aisle and helped lift him up onto the stage, where he stood awkwardly, obviously a bit stage-struck.

I gave him a huge hug. 'Isn't this perfect?' I said. 'All best friends together?'

Miranda looked at Arnie and laughed.

'At least your "army" won't throw things at us while you're up here. And nothing can spoil the feeling of having my friends up

here with me. ♪ **BEST FRIENDS FOREVER!** ♪'

Danny, Frank, and I joined her in a group
hug and sang, '♪ **BEST FRIENDS FOREVER!** ♪'

When Miranda released us, I grabbed
Danny and Frank and, like a team of not-
very-synchronized synchronized swimmers,
we all leapt into Miranda's tank, cheering
and yelling, 'We'll make sure you go out
with a SPLASH!'

Frank was last to
dive in. He got
squished at the

top and wedged us all into the tank.

It made it hard to bow, but fortunately, the stage hands managed to pry us out with the theatre's lifting hoist just in time for Miranda to receive her first standing ovation.

Greetings, beloved parents,

Hope you are well and life in Story Land is full of cupcakes and rainbows.

Everything is marvellous here in New York. As you know, all my friends are stars to me, but this term, my friend Miranda the Mermaid became a real-life superstar, with her face on posters, her tail on T-shirts, and her life plastered all over the magazines and newspapers. Although that last one is far less fun than you might think. Newspapers can be mean and the news is not always the same as the truth.

I learned it's sometimes hard to be a good friend. It can leave you smelling of tomatoes, or dangling by your horn from a fancy apartment door. But it's always worth it. There is nothing more important than friendship.

My new theory is that friendship is like a pencil case. You need glue to stick together in the tough times. You need colouring pens to create the good times, and you need Tippex to delete any bad bits from your mind. I tried to share this theory with my friends, but they told me to stop talking and get on with setting up the glitter ball for our next party, because that's what friendship is really all about.

They are probably right.

Love you more than cake,

Louie Xxxx

Oscar Armelles was born in Spain, and almost from day one, could be found with a pen and paper in his hand, he loved to draw—anything and everything. As soon as he was old enough, he collected all his crayons and moved to America where he studied Commercial Art.

After graduating, he relocated to London and now he spends his time coming and going between London and Madrid.

He works mainly in digital format . . . although he is quite handy with watercolours too.

Rachel Hamilton studied at both Oxford and Cambridge and has put her education to good use working in an ad agency, a secondary school, a building site, and a men's prison. Her interests are books, films, stand-up comedy, and cake, and she loves to make people laugh, especially when it's intentional rather than accidental.

Rachel is currently working on the *Unicorn in New York* series for OUP and divides her time between the UK and the UAE, where she enjoys making up funny stories for 7 to 13 year olds.

LOOK OUT FOR MORE ADVENTURES WITH LOUIE THE UNICORN.

Unicorn in New York

LOUIE LETS LOOSE!

It's time for this unicorn to shine!

RACHEL HAMILTON

Illustrated by OSCAR ARMELLES

LOUIE THE UNICORN LEAVES STORY LAND TO BEGIN HIS SEARCH FOR STARDOM IN NEW YORK CITY, FIRST STOP, PERFORMING ARTS SCHOOL!

Unicorn in New York

LOUIE
TAKES THE STAGE!

It's time for this unicorn to shine!

I ♥ NY

Illustrated by
OSCAR ARMELLES

RACHEL HAMILTON

LOUIE JOINED THE NEW YORK SCHOOL
OF PERFORMING ARTS IN SEARCH OF
STARDOM, BUT HE'S YET TO LAND ANY
STARRING ROLES, WITH A BIG AUDITION
COMING UP, IS IT FINALLY TIME FOR THIS
UNICORN TO SHINE?

LOUIE'S DANCE MOVES ALWAYS END
IN DISASTER, SO WHEN HE MISTAKENLY
GETS ENTERED INTO A STATE-WIDE
DANCE CONTEST HE'S GOING TO
HAVE TO GIVE IT HIS ALL FOR A
CHANCE OF WINNING.

HERE ARE SOME OTHER STORIES THAT WE THINK YOU'LL LOVE.